# THIS DIARY BELONGS TO
## Eliza Boom

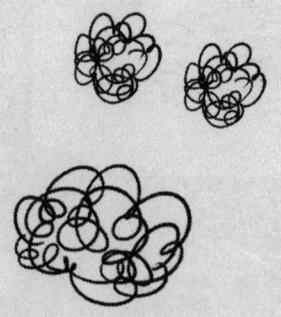

# Eliza Boom

# my explosive diary

BY Emily Gale

ILLUSTRATED BY Joëlle Dreidemy

Aladdin * NEW YORK  LONDON  TORONTO  SYDNEY  NEW DELHI

# With special thanks to
# Justine Smith and Hannah Cohen

## ALADDIN

An imprint of Simon & Schuster Children's Publishing Division
1230 Avenue of the Americas, New York, NY 10020
First Aladdin paperback edition July 2014
Text copyright © 2014 by Emily Gale
Interior illustrations copyright © 2014 by Buster Books
Originally published as *Eliza Boom: The Explosive Adventure*
in 2014 in Great Britain by Buster Books
Cover illustrations copyright © 2014 by Joëlle Dreidemy
All rights reserved, including the right of reproduction in whole or in part in any form.
ALADDIN is a trademark of Simon & Schuster, Inc., and related logo
is a registered trademark of Simon & Schuster, Inc.
For information about special discounts for bulk purchases, please contact
Simon & Schuster Special Sales at 1-866-506-1949 or business@simonandschuster.com.
The Simon & Schuster Speakers Bureau can bring authors to your live event. For more information
or to book an event contact the Simon & Schuster Speakers Bureau at 1-866-248-3049 or visit
our website at www.simonspeakers.com.
Cover designed by Karin Paprocki
The text of this book was set in Brandon Grotesque.
Manufactured in the United States of America 0614 OFF
2 4 6 8 10 9 7 5 3 1
Library of Congress Control Number 2013956389
ISBN 978-1-4814-0650-5 (hc)
ISBN 978-1-4814-0648-2 (pbk)
ISBN 978-1-4814-0651-2 (eBook)

# Saturday Night
## My Lab, 7 p.m.

Dear Diary,

We've been banished to the lab FOREVER.
You'll understand why when I tell you about
my latest invention.

That's me, Eliza.

That's my dog,
Einstein.

It was Invention 92: the Super-Sneaky
Spy-Cam Collar.

Invention 92
(modeled by
Einstein)

Shiny!

Useful!

Brilliant!

2

This is what happened to it.

Don't worry, Einstein wasn't wearing it at the time.

Dad says that before every good invention there are 99 not-so-good ones. That was number 92. I'm SO CLOSE, Diary.

Everyone in my family had the grumps after the explosion.

Not again, Eliza!

Alice, my stepmom (super-mad, as usual)

Dad (mad)

Plum, my baby sister (mad, but still cute)

Einstein is the only one who has forgiven me.

He understands me even if no one else does.

This is him.

My best friend

He loves wearing his lab coat.
Seriously, he does.

I named him Einstein after the real Einstein,
who was a scientist. But he's dead now. Not my
dog—the scientist.

Do you know what hurt the most?

It was what Dad said:

Go to your BEDROOM
this instant, Eliza!

He knows I don't have a bedroom. I have a
LAB. Bedrooms are just for sleeping in. I'm
too busy inventing to sleep!

Dad has a lab too, only his is disguised as a garden shed.

Never judge a shed by its cover.

Dad is a fully qualified inventor who makes gadgets for spies, and I'm his assistant. I like being an assistant inventor, but one day I'd actually like to be a SPY, too. I mean, why should someone ELSE get to have all the fun with MY inventions?

Speaking of inventions, how did my Super-Sneaky Spy-Cam Collar go so wrong? It would have been PERFECT for tracking down where Einstein buries our things . . .

Me, inventing the Super-Sneaky Spy-Cam Collar

... like Alice's shoes,

... Plum's toys,

... and even Dad's tools

from his tool belt.

I showed Alice my invention yesterday
before it exploded. She should have been
super-impressed, but she barely looked at it.
That was very non-super of her.

No one cares about any of my inventions—especially Alice. All she cares about is her garden. That's why she confiscated Invention 91: the Spy Rocket that I invented last week. She just doesn't understand me or my inventions.

Alice, Chief Inventor of a Boring Rosebush

Invention 91 (crashed)

My plan was to make Einstein wear his Super-Sneaky Spy-Cam Collar, and then I'd watch the film to see where his secret stash was buried.

But when I connected the Super-Sneaky Spy-Cam to the telecommunication system (the TV) via the electric current carrier (the TV cable), and put on our flying particle protectors (goggles) . . . well, you know what happened:

And that brings us back to right now.

I'm desperate to come up with an even better
invention. That's why we're upside down—it
helps you think. It also makes your hair grow,
which is probably why we both have big,
fuzzy hairstyles.

Thinking . . . thinking . . . I just know something
will come to me soon.

Yours inventively,
Eliza Boom
Inventor-in-Training

**P.S.** Since I'm writing my inventions in your pages, Diary, you should have a scientific name, too.

I name this diary "Edison."

Edison invented this:

**That's a lightbulb, by the way, not a worm.**

# Sunday Night
## My Lab, 9 p.m. ← *Busy day!*

Dear Edison,

All that thinking has led to my new Diva-Pro Ultra-Heated Hair Rollers invention.

**Invention 93, please prove Dad wrong and WORK!**

*Hair this wild needs SCIENCE.*

Everything was going well until . . .

**MINI BOOM!**

. . . our rollers exploded and Einstein ran away.

I quickly took my rollers out and went looking for him. In the hallway I caught sight of my hair.

I looked more like a Golden Retriever than a Super-Cool Diva!

*Woof?*

Using hair clips, I performed vital emergency surgery and soon the search for Einstein was back on . . .

. . . which led me to Dad's shed.

When I got inside, things did NOT look good.

Dad was crying and trying to tear out his hair.
Which is hard to do when you're already bald.

There seemed to be a problem with Dad's amazing MindReader2000.

It wasn't reading minds. THIS WAS SERIOUS! If it can't read minds, The MindReader2000 is just a very ugly hat.

By now, Dad had done so much crying he had the hiccups. Being an inventor is very stressful.

Dad needed urgent
help, and I was it.

BOOM!

First, I got rid of
his hiccups.

Then I had a good look at The MindReader2000.
Fortunately, I had my tool belt and headlamp
with me.

Right away I spotted
the problem: a loose
screw in a tiny hole.
I was going to need
a very special tool to
remove it . . .

The hair clip

Happy Dad

A HAIR CLIP!

Easy-peasy.

Dad was grateful, but instead of asking me to
help some more, he said I had to go.

SUSPICIOUS!

Why was he in such a hurry to get rid of me? It was time to do some spying of my own.

I scratched a peephole in the blacked-out window of his shed.

Dad was at his computer. There was a shadowy figure on the screen. It must have been Dad's Spy Boss, the one in charge of all the spies.

The voice coming out was low and rumbly like a robot running out of battery. I could only make out two words:

MISSION . . . METALLIC

Suddenly, Einstein appeared at my side, and we had to make a getaway before Dad caught us.

We ran straight back to my lab, and I removed Einstein's Diva-Pro rollers.

He was very upset by the results. Sorry, my furry friend. I had to spend the rest of the night comforting him.

He wanted a never-ending tummy rub. But I had work to do if I was going to figure out how to get Dad to take me seriously as an inventor and introduce me to his Spy Boss.

So I invented something that would occupy
Einstein:

**Invention 94:
the Never-Ending
Tummy Rubber
(Please work so
I can show Dad!)**

Yours inventively,
Eliza Boom
Assistant Inventor

P.S. I can't stop thinking about
MISSION METALLIC. . . .

# Monday Morning
## My Lab, 7 a.m.

Dear Edison,

Good news: As Einstein snored next to me,
I woke up at 4 a.m. with an invention buzzing
around in my head.

It was a present for Dad, to make sure he
never has trouble with tiny screws messing up
his brilliant machines.

METHOD:

Glue five super-strong magnets on to one of
Alice's pink rubber gloves (thanks, Alice).

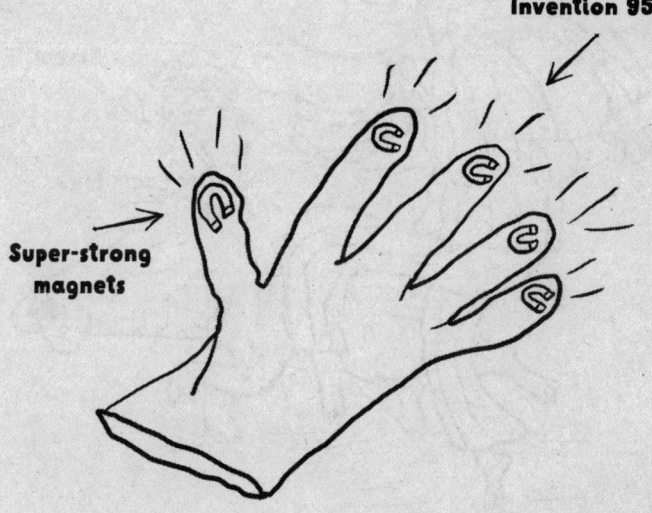

Invention 95

Super-strong
magnets

And there you have it . . .
the Magno-Glove!

Testing inventions is really important. The sun wasn't up yet, but I couldn't wait. I tiptoed round the house wearing the Magno-Glove.

Teaspoon

Screw

Fork

It was going great until . . .

. . . I accidentally woke up Plum. Her
screeching made Einstein start to howl . . .

. . . which woke up the rest of the house.

That's when Alice busted me.

Eliza Boom, is that my rubber glove?
Hand it over, young lady.

There was only one way those magnets were coming off. SNIP! Well, I couldn't give away my super-powerful magnets, could I?

This is what the glove looked like when I gave it back.

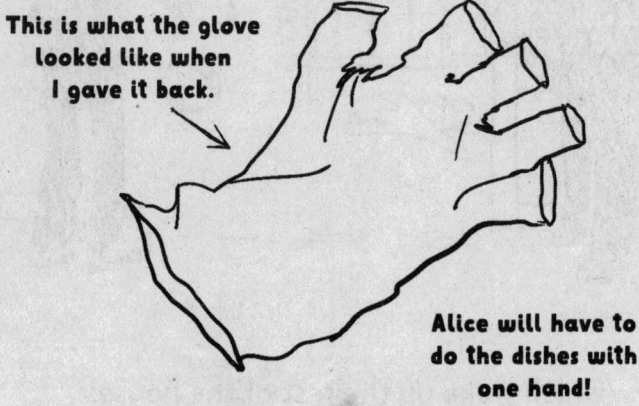

Alice will have to do the dishes with one hand!

Dad sent everyone back to bed, but I couldn't sleep.

I lay awake thinking about school, and how much easier my life would be if Zoe Wakefield was nicer.

ZOE WAKEFIELD, Class Meanie

Mean Mouth Machine (where all her horrible comments come out)

Perfect hair, of course

Heart made of stone

The more I thought about
Zoe, the more knotted
my tummy became. I get
that way after I've eaten
dairy, too.

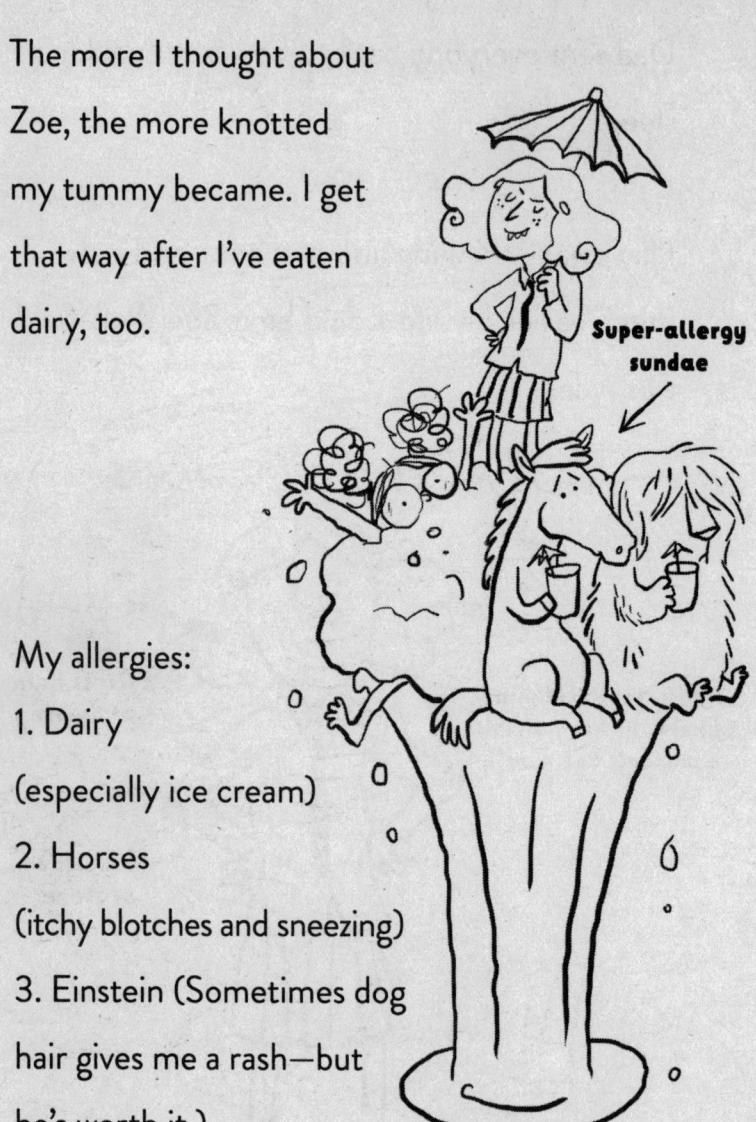

Super-allergy
sundae

My allergies:

1. Dairy
(especially ice cream)
2. Horses
(itchy blotches and sneezing)
3. Einstein (Sometimes dog
hair gives me a rash—but
he's worth it.)

And finally, the worst allergy of all:

**4.** ZOE WAKEFIELD, Queen of Mean.

Zoe being mean to me isn't new. But she's having a party this week and I CAN'T be the only kid not invited.

Don't worry, Edison. I've got a plan: What if I give Zoe a present BEFORE her birthday? She'll have to invite me then! And what if it's something as amazing as THIS?

A STAR IN A JAR!

Invention 96

STEP 1:
Take one jar.

## STEP 2:

Measure and cut some fishing wire.

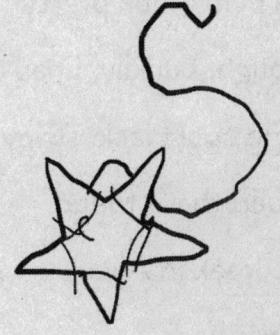

## STEP 3:

Tie a beautiful star to one end.

## STEP 4:

Stick the fishing wire to the inside of the lid with a super-strong magnet.

It's impossible to look at it and not say,

"OOOOH."

I wrapped the jar in some homemade wrapping paper, but it still didn't look pretty enough. Luckily, I had some cool black, stripy ribbon that I found last week in Alice's flower beds.

**Einstein thinks it's pretty!**

I just know I'm going to win Zoe's heart with this invention, and get an invitation to her party.

Sorry, Edison, I've got to go. Alice is shouting, "School time!" It's always "Something-Time" with Alice.

**Before I go, here's how we look after being up all night inventing.**

Yours inventively,
Eliza Boom
24-Hour Inventor

# Monday Night
## My Lab, 5 p.m.

Dear Edison,

Bad news! When I got to school, I found out that everyone in my class had the same idea about a pre-birthday birthday present for Zoe.

Zoe made us line up so she could inspect the presents. It was so embarrassing.

It was like being at an audition in front of the world's most evil judge. Nobody's present was good enough for Zoe.

I've got two of those already.

It was my turn next.

I held my breath as Zoe took off the ribbon and
unwrapped the jar.

This is what she said:

My daddy named a
REAL star after me
when I was five. It's
bigger than the sun.
LOSER!

# AAAAAAAARGHHHHHH!

She hated my invention. It was a disaster.

So I asked Zoe for the jar back, and the weird
ribbon that I'd found in Alice's flower beds
(I knew Einstein would appreciate it!), but Zoe
had other ideas.

She took the ribbon and tied it into her perfect
hair and put the jar in her bag.

Wow, did that mean she was going to invite me
to her party after all?

Zoe sat down to write down the names of all the kids she was inviting and then all the kids not invited.

She stuck the list on the wall and left the classroom, chucking my beautiful, handmade wrapping paper in the trash as she went.

Everyone rushed over to find their name.

INVITED

Almost the entire human race.

NOT INVITED

Eliza Boom

Amy Madden, a.k.a. Mayo-Amy

What's so wrong with me and Mayo-Amy? Amy's new this year. I hardly know her (I'm usually too busy inventing to make friends). But I do know that Amy's hair got washed in MAYONNAISE by her mom to get rid of lice.

Poor Amy: Her mom thought she was a salad.

Everyone says she smells eggy. That's probably why she's not invited either.

As for me, what a waste of a good invention!

Now Zoe has one of my super-strong magnets, and it was all for nothing. I felt just like the scrunched-up wrapping paper she'd thrown in the trash.

I came home to more disaster. Dad was pulling

the place apart, looking for something.

HELP ME, ELIZA!
I've lost my new invention:
the Mission Metallic Info-Ribbon.

What does it look
like, Dad?

Like a reel!

A real
what?

NO! A REEL!
A film reel!

Poor Dad. He'd fitted his new invention with a tracking device, but that had gone missing too!

Einstein promised he hadn't buried it, and what else could I do but believe him? After all, he is my best friend.

**Who could resist this face?**

Dad looked everywhere, and I helped.

Then Plum waddled in, dressed like a tiger with a very long, stripy tail.

Dad grabbed Plum by the tail.

It's long and black and stripy like this! Only it's actually a piece of METALLIC RIBBON and contains TOP-SECRET SPY INFORMATION! Anyone seen it? AAANNNYYYONE?

OH, EDISON! That's when I realized! And
I ran to my lab to hide under the covers, where
I plan to stay, minding my own business for the
rest of my life. Don't ask me why, Edison.

JUST DON'T!

Fine, you win! I'll tell you.

The ribbon I used on Zoe's present isn't ribbon at all. Remember how I said I found it in Alice's flower beds? And remember how strange it was? That's because it isn't ribbon—it's Dad's invention!

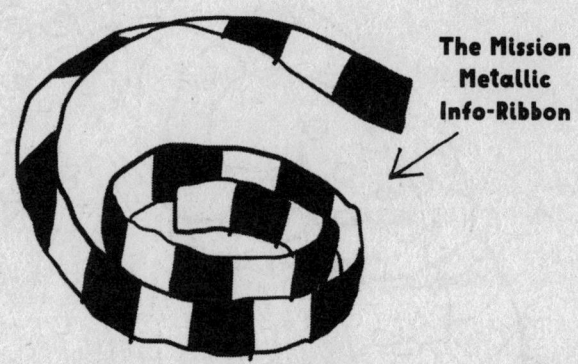

**The Mission Metallic Info-Ribbon**

SO ALL THOSE SECRET SPY MESSAGES . . . ARE IN ZOE WAKEFIELD'S HAIR!

Dad could lose his job over this! Which means I would lose mine!

Edison, somehow, despite my best intentions and brilliant inventions, I've created:

AN INTERNATIONAL EMERGENCY!

So, I've decided I can't hide in my lab.

I'll go to school tomorrow and demand the ribbon back from Zoe.

Dad needs me. The world needs me!

Yours guiltily,
Eliza Boom
Inventor-in-Trouble

# Tuesday Night
## My Lab, 7 p.m.

Dear Edison,

As soon as I got to school, I pleaded with Zoe to give the ribbon back.

Only if you say, "Please, please, please, Zoe, you are awesome and I, Eliza Boom, am a L.O.S.E.R."

And she wasn't joking. I had to make myself
picture Dad last night in utter despair just so
I could get the words out. But I did it, Edison.
And then she said . . .

NO.

I was so angry I thought
my eyeballs would pop
out of my face.

I felt someone's hand give my shoulder a gentle squeeze. It was Mayo-Amy. That made me feel a tiny bit better, but then I thought I was going to cry, so I ran out of the classroom.

I went to my special thinking place:

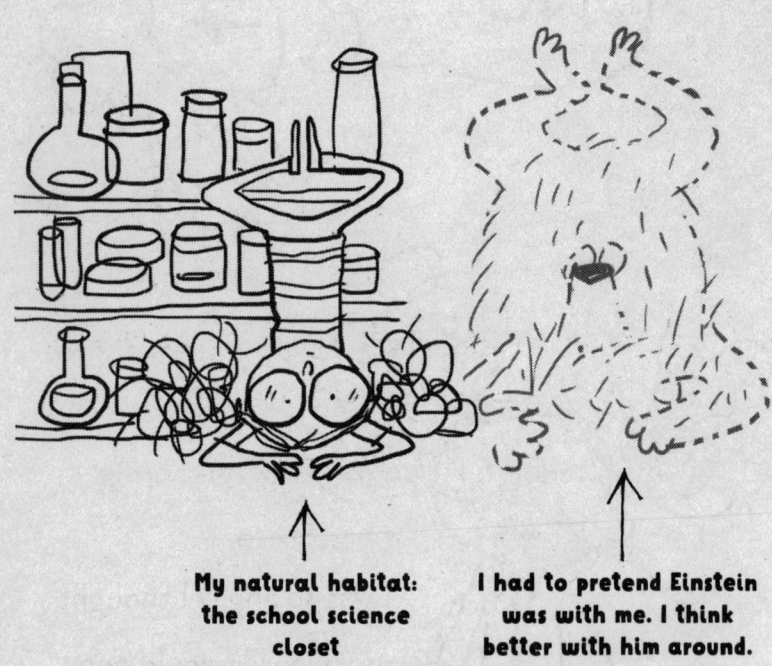

**My natural habitat: the school science closet**

**I had to pretend Einstein was with me. I think better with him around.**

I had to make my brain work extra-hard to figure out how to get the ribbon back.

**My extra-hard-working brain**

THINKING . . .

THINKING . . .

There is so much useful stuff for junior inventors in that closet. It was giving me ideas just looking at all those tubes and clips and things. I thought: if I borrow them and bring them back later, I might be able to . . .

. . . SAVE THE WORLD! Plus Dad!

Good old brain. In a flash it came up with Invention 97.

**This is Invention 97: the Grabber**

I stuffed my new invention down the back of my shirt and hurried to class.

I was really late!

Ms. Bacon did not look happy.

But that was the least of my worries, because the next thing I knew . . .

I was flying!

When I crash-landed, I looked back to see Zoe's gigantic foot in the way.

She had tripped me!

The worst part was that the Grabber had fallen out, and Ms. Bacon didn't believe my story about borrowing school equipment to save humankind.

So I'd lost the Grabber and I was off to see Principal Bixley. I'm scared of Principal Bixley. She always smells like cheese, and you know how I get around dairy.

Sit there and think about your actions, Eliza Boom.

I did exactly as I was told. I sat there and thought about what actions I needed to take to get that ribbon off Zoe Wakefield's horrible head.

At dismissal, the weirdest thing happened.

I was standing with Mayo-Amy when Zoe

Wakefield ... SMILED AT US.

I've decided you can both come to my party after all. It's a costume party, and whoever wins best costume gets to take home WHATEVER THEY WANT.

Then she touched the ribbon and winked at me.

"Whatever they want ..." BRILLIANT!

All I've got to do is invent the best costume and

I'll ask for the "ribbon" back. (If I tell Zoe it's a

brilliant invention, she'll never let me have it!)

Yours inventively,
Eliza Boom
Costume-Inventor Extraordinaire

# Tuesday Night
## Still in the Lab, 9:30 p.m.

Dear Edison,

The BAD NEWS is...

I asked Dad just how much trouble we'd be in
if we never got the ribbon back. He couldn't
even speak. He just croaked a bit and held out
his arms as wide as he could.

THIS MUCH TROUBLE!

# The GOOD NEWS is...

I've designed a costume so amazing that the next time I see Dad I'll be making him the happiest inventor alive.

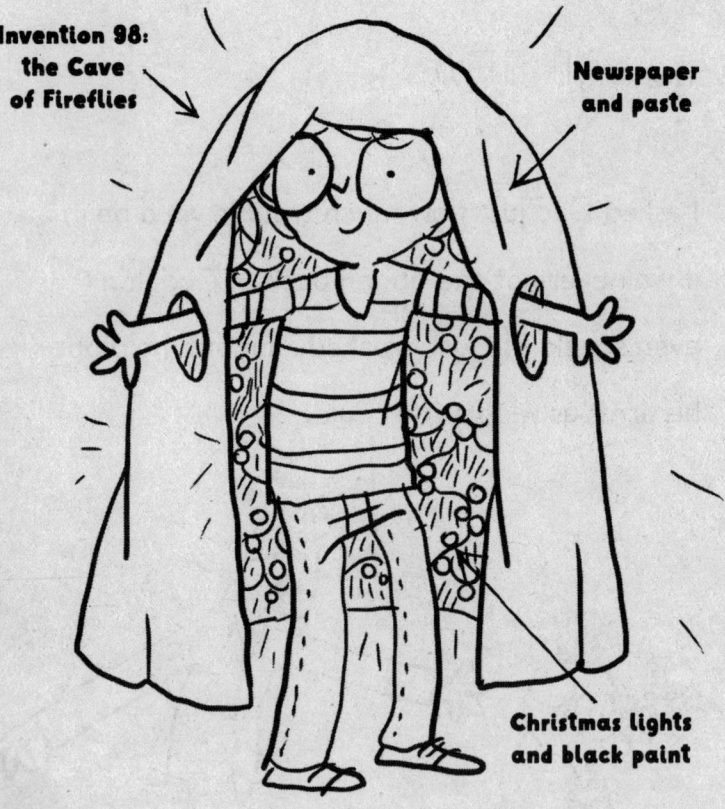

**Invention 98: the Cave of Fireflies**

**Newspaper and paste**

**Christmas lights and black paint**

Papier-mâché + electronic genius =
I'M A CAVE ... OF FIREFLIES!

Einstein loves it so much he's going to sleep in it all night.

I'm sure my sparkly cave invention will win best costume.

Yours hopefully,
Eliza Boom
Inventerrific!

# Wednesday Night
## My Lab, 8:30 p.m.

Dear Edison,

I'm back from Zoe Wakefield's party, feeling just like Cinderella when she got home from the ball.

It's no use, Edison, I can't lie to you. Actually, I feel NOTHING LIKE CINDERELLA.

The main difference is that Cinderella turned up in a beautiful dress and the crowd gasped.

Whereas I, Eliza Boom, turned up as a cave, while poor Mayo-Amy turned up as a dog, and everyone LAUGHED. BECAUSE IT WASN'T A COSTUME PARTY AFTER ALL!

I was upset, but I had to pull myself together.
Zoe had Dad's secret spy ribbon in her hair,
and I wasn't leaving until I had it back.

Zoe's mom helped me take off the cave so I could
join in the "special activity" they had planned.

I noticed Mayo-Amy checking the costume
out. She looked impressed, but I tried not to
let that distract me.

It was time for the "special activity."

Mrs. Wakefield told everyone to go out into the garden.

I followed Zoe, wondering what the "special activity" could be. . . .

This was it. Horses—why did it have to be horses?

My worst nightmare

Zoe told us the horses' names: Dancer, Prancer, Frisky, Mary, and Daisy.

Inside my head I quickly renamed them all: Danger, Double-Danger, Risky, Scary, and Crazy.

There was a big, hairy horse lady standing in front of those evil snorting beasts.

**She looked like she ate horses for breakfast!**

Zoe got on the
white one: Dancer,
a.k.a. Danger.

She made us wait ages while she picked riders
for the other horses.

Unlike the other kids, Mayo-Amy was trying
to hide. I started to think we had a few things
in common.

Of course, I didn't need to hide because Zoe
would never pick me for anything.

I think Zoe's next words were:

Eliza, I pick you
to ride Daisy.

But this is what I heard:

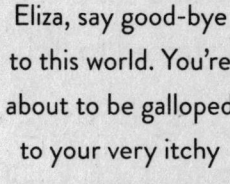

Eliza, say good-bye
to this world. You're
about to be galloped
to your very itchy

DEATH!

Edison, SHE PICKED ME! Zoe knew
about my allergies and my very real fear of
horses. What happened next is too horrible to
talk about.

But I will.

The hairy horse lady picked me up and put me on Crazy-Daisy, whose tail was swishing like it hated me already.

I started to itch.

But when I tried to tell the hairy horse lady about my allergy, she didn't seem to hear me. She was staring at Zoe's hair.

First we walked around a bit. I think we did, anyway. I had my eyes closed.

Then I heard Zoe say "FASTER!" and just like everyone else on the planet, the horses obeyed her.

## "TROT!"

Trotting was horrible. It felt like a punishment!
Maybe I deserved one for giving Zoe the spy
ribbon and getting Dad into trouble.

Meanwhile, Zoe was showing off, and that's
when I saw my chance.

I shimmied up my horse's neck and reached out to get a bit closer...

CLOSER...

CLOSER...

Almost there!

... but then I got distracted by the hairy horse lady, who still seemed interested in Zoe's ribbon too, and...

... all I remember next is seeing Zoe's face in the sky, the ribbon STILL in her hair, and me landing like THIS:

THUD!

The next party activity was a bouncy castle, but I was still feeling bruised from my fall. I stayed in the kitchen and watched the food coming out.

The cake was a huge pink castle with a girl made of marzipan who looked exactly like Zoe.

I picked up some tongs from the table and thought about knocking the head right off that mean marzipan girl.

But that's when a plan came to me. I'd use the tongs to get the ribbon out of Zoe's hair while she was blowing out her candles!

With everyone back inside and ready for cake, and a dish towel draped over my arm to conceal the tongs, my new plan was working . . .

. . . until Zoe said:

Mommy, don't forget the special dessert for Eliza. She's allergic to cake.

I dropped the tongs!

Before I knew it, I was face-to-face with
another of my nightmares.

ICE CREAM.

Mrs. Wakefield seemed so nice—how could
I tell her that ice cream makes me puke?

You think this diary entry will end in misery,
Edison, but you're wrong. A surprise
SOMEONE came to my rescue.

Mayo-Amy!

She grabbed the spoon and saved me before
my very eyes.

And that's when I realized that Mayo-Amy had
to be part of my next plan.

The plan had two parts:

1. Stop calling Mayo-Amy "Mayo-Amy." Even though it's only in my head.

2. Ask Amy to be my new assistant. Assistant to the Assistant to the Inventor for International Espionage (that means spying). AAIIE for short.

I told Amy about the plan. She thought about part two of the plan for a moment and then said:

You need an assistant and I need a best friend. Deal?

**Yes, you read that right, Edison . . . she wants to be my friend too.** YAY!

Before we left the party, I told Amy all about the spy ribbon containing secret information.

She was shocked. She's coming to my house before school tomorrow to help me invent a new gadget to get the ribbon back for real this time.

I'm excited, Edison! But now I have to lie down. I'm aching all over after that death-defying ride on Crazy-Daisy.

Yours, covered in bruises,
Eliza Boom
Assistant Inventor
(who also has an assistant!)

**Frozen peas**

# Thursday Night
## My Lab, 7 p.m.

Dear Edison,

Amy was here by 7 a.m. I love how dedicated she is.

First I introduced her to Einstein. They're going to get along really well. . . .

**Amy loves dogs!**

It turns out that Amy and I have loads more in common.

Amy is terrified of horses too.
And she has an allergy. Pineapples.

Killer pineapple

Killer horse

Our new idea is really one of my old ideas, only much better.

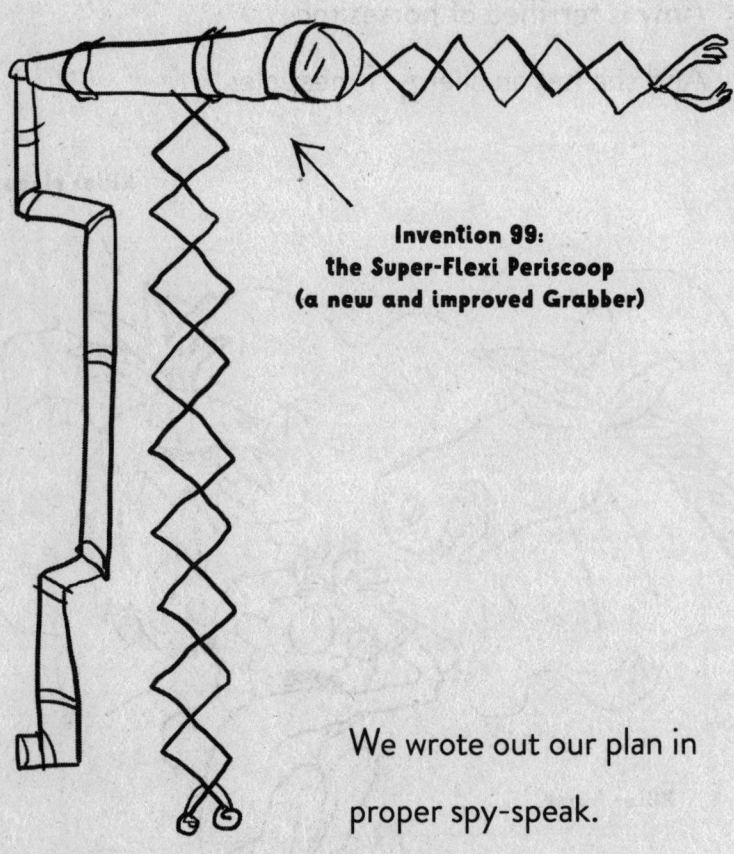

**Invention 99:**
**the Super-Flexi Periscoop**
**(a new and improved Grabber)**

We wrote out our plan in proper spy-speak.

THE PLAN:

Locate "Enemy 1" (Zoe!)

Camouflage special agents (hide!)

Assemble hardware
(aim the Super-Flexi Periscoop!)

Identify cargo (check she's wearing
the ribbon!)

Activate weapon (grab the ribbon!)

Evacuate scene (run!)

We raided the kitchen and Dad's lab for extra supplies in case we needed to invent something on the go.

Then we changed into special spy clothes and tried to carry as many of my inventions as we could, including the Diva-Pro Hair Rollers (you never know), and the glove fingers with super-strong magnets on (left over from the Magno-Glove).

**Super-shades for super-spies** →

Before we left for school, Amy and I said good-bye to Einstein, who was feeling sad about being left behind.

Poor Einy . . .

So I gave him one of Alice's shoes as a special treat (it's okay, he'd already buried the other one, so it was no good to Alice anymore).

All the kids were out in the playground before school started. We were in a perfect position . . .

. . . until BRRRRRRRR! The school bell rang—FIVE MINUTES EARLY!

**ALL STUDENTS TO THE AUDITORIUM FOR FULL INSPECTION!**

We'd never had a full inspection before. No one knew what it could mean. What were they looking for? Lice? Chicken pox? Lipstick? Candy?

All Amy and I cared about was that it was interrupting our plan.

In the auditorium, Principal Bixley came onstage.

Right away I noticed what everyone else seemed to have missed (I was born to be a spy):

It wasn't the R E A L Principal Bixley! For one thing, she was giant-size, with a beard.

That's when it hit me, Edison. The hairy horse lady from Zoe's party and this principal were THE SAME PERSON! A HOSTILE INFILTRATOR, as we say in the spy trade.

Real principal

Phony principal

Hairy horse lady

Then, Fake
Principal
Bixley made an
announcement:

Owing to a health and safety issue,
pupils will have to remove all hair items
immediately. Hair bands, hair ties, hair clips,
hair elastics, hair bobbins, and any other
hair hardware. Especially hair ribbons.
MOVE IT!

The room went wild. I nudged Amy and waited
for her to see that this was all a trick. . . .

It didn't take her long to figure it out. The trouble was, we didn't know what to do next.

Zoe Wakefield was having a tantrum about how long she'd spent doing her hair that morning. WITH MY SPY RIBBON, OF COURSE!

I won't take it out! I won't, I won't, I won't! This perfect hair took me three hours!

Three hours? I couldn't help wondering if Zoe styled her hair with her feet—why else would it take that long?

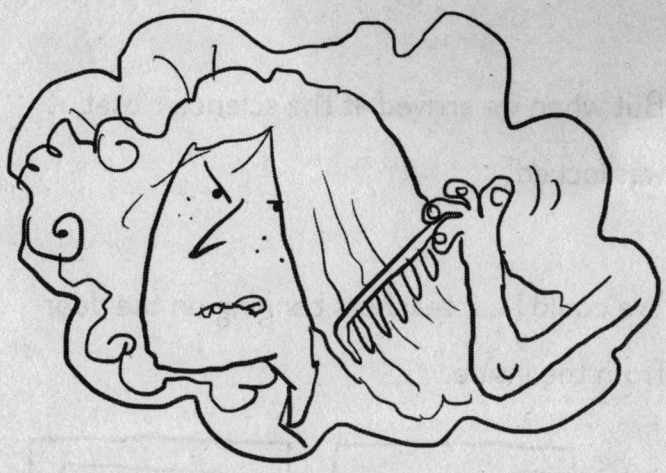

Despite Zoe's tantrum, the spy ribbon went into a huge bag that was being passed around. Soon after, the bag and Fake Principal Bixley had DISAPPEARED!

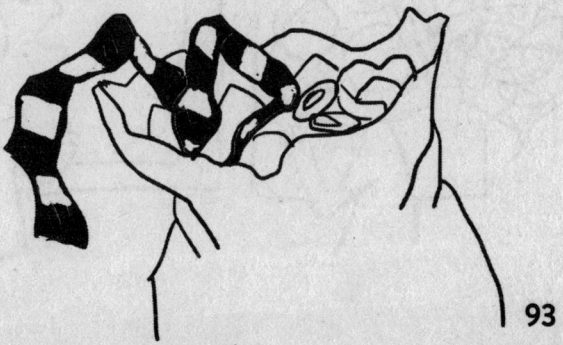

We were being outsmarted! I didn't like it one bit. So I took Amy to my special thinking place.

But when we arrived at the science closet, it was locked!

We could hear teachers banging on the door from the inside.

Then I heard Real Principal Bixley's voice through the door.

Eliza Boom! Do not use explosives! I repeat: NO EXPLOSIVES!

That did it. If Real Principal Bixley was going to bring up things FROM THE PAST, I'd leave her in there and continue on the hunt for Fake Principal Bixley (F.P.B.).

We had to find F.P.B. before the spy ribbon was gone for good. We got going right away.

On the way, I had an idea. Dad had told me his spy ribbon invention was metallic. What if I used one of the super-strong magnets from Invention 95, formerly known as the Magno-Glove?

You could dangle a magnet into the F.P.B.'s bag with the Super-Flexi Periscoop!

Just what I was thinking, Amy!

Now we just had to find the bag.

But guess who
showed up to
block our way!

**Zoe and her
meanie friends** →

Ideas were coming to me so fast I could barely
keep up with them. I gave Zoe my Diva-Pro
Ultra-Heated Hair Rollers to distract her.

She didn't know whether to fix her hair or keep
being mean to me. Finally her hair won, and
Amy and I were on our way again.

We ran outside and around to the principal's office window to see if the F.P.B. was using it as a base.

Do you see what I see, Amy?

Yes! It's hairy horse lady Fake Principal Bixley!

Then we crouched down to make some important changes to the Super-Flexi Periscoop, using some wire, lots of duct tape, and one of my super-strong magnets.

**Invention 100
(according to Dad, this one
really will work!)**

**The New and Improved
Super-Flexi MAGNO-Periscoop**

I peered through the window again. The bag was in full view. So was the F.P.B., who had now changed out of HIS disguise.

Yes, you read that right, Edison . . . the F.P.B./hairy horse lady wasn't a lady at all!

This is Mole 1. Operation nearly complete. Back to base at 1300 hours.

He was talking into his watch.

We had to act fast, but I was worried the
Super-Flexi Magno-Periscoop might not be
long enough to reach into the
bag and pick up the ribbon.

I told Amy to hold on to
my legs.

I WAS GOING IN!

I was hardly breathing as I found myself looking down on Mole 1. While he was fiddling with his spy-watch, I started to lower the magnet toward the bag.

Closer ... CLOSER ...
CLOSER ...

But then Mole 1 bent over the bag! And before I could stop it, the super-strong magnet had attached itself to his belt.

He started to spin around and around, trying to see what he was attached to. I held on tight to the Super-Flexi Magno-Periscoop, but I could feel the wire unraveling more and more, and Amy's hands were almost slipping off my ankles. . . .

# AAAARGHHHHHHHHH!

The next thing we knew, I'd fallen into the room and brought Amy with me.

But when we stood up, we saw something amazing.

Mole 1 was completely tangled up in the wire from our Super-Flexi Magno-Periscoop!

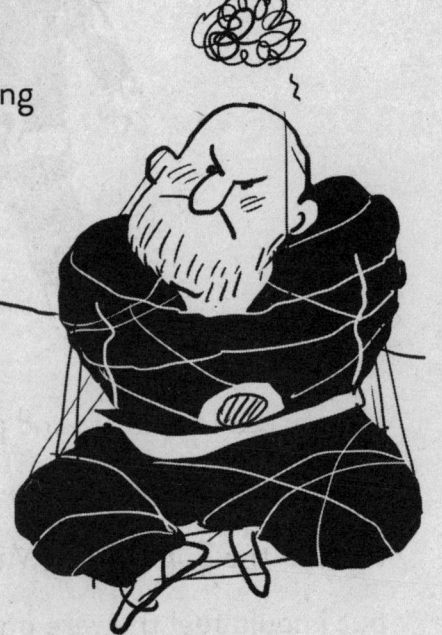

I grabbed the ribbon out of the bag.

Then I did something that felt just as good:
I hugged my brilliant assistant (and new human
best friend!), Amy.

Just as we were securing Mole 1, the door was kicked in.

And I couldn't believe who came rushing in . . .

. . . Alice, Dad, Plum . . . and Einstein!

Edison, I'll give you a moment to let all of that sink in.

All right, that's long enough. I have so much more to tell you!

Alice stepped forward and took the ribbon from my hands and put it in her pocket.

Nice work, Eliza. As if finding the spy ribbon wasn't enough, you caught a dangerous enemy spy. His team has been trying to get their hands on this information for years.

I couldn't understand it. Alice usually says things like: "Go to bed, Eliza" and "Eat your peas, Eliza."

How did she know about this spy stuff?

Then she shook my hand and said something
even more strange.

Senior Agent Electra at your service.
I'm pleased to inform you that your
one hundredth invention has just saved
Mission Metallic!

I can't remember exactly what I said, but
I think it was something like:

HUH?

I asked Dad how they'd tracked me—and the ribbon—to Principal Bixley's office.

It was Einstein!
He buried my missing tracking device for the spy ribbon in his special burying place—where I found everything else he's buried. The tracking device led us here!

# GOOD DOG!

I told you he was a genius!

Alice, a.k.a. Senior
Agent Electra, put her
arm around me.

And home is where I am right now, Edison.
Amy's here too, for a sleepover, and she's even
brought her dog.

**Amy's dog, Luna**

I'd better go. I'll explain more tomorrow.

Yours triumphantly,
Eliza Boom
Assistant Inventor and Enemy Spy Capturer!

P.S. Alice is still my stepmom. She just leads a double life. She and Dad work together, and SHE (Alice) was the shadowy figure I saw on the computer screen in Dad's shed/lab.

AWESOME!

Alice, stepmom

Alice, a.k.a. Spy Boss

# Friday Morning
## My Lab, 7 a.m.

Dear Edison,

Six brilliant things:

1. Dad's job is safe.

**Dad's happy thoughts!**

Eliza saved the day!

My genius MindReader2000 reads minds again. YES!!

I want pancakes for breakfast.

2. Alice said she wanted to show me something special. But when she took me to her prize rosebush, I was disappointed. I was about to explain how boring gardening is, when . . .

Best rosebush EVER!

. . . a trapdoor opened up and Alice led me to her secret underground spy HQ!

Things could not get better than that ... oh, wait, they could!

Brilliant thing number 3 is that school is closed for a little holiday.

Yesterday, Amy remembered that all the teachers were locked up, and we went back to rescue them.

We can't go back to school until the security
has been investigated. That could take weeks!

My school,
CLOSED!

Which means more time for my inventions,
including . . .

. . . brilliant thing number 4: Egg-Away Shampoo.

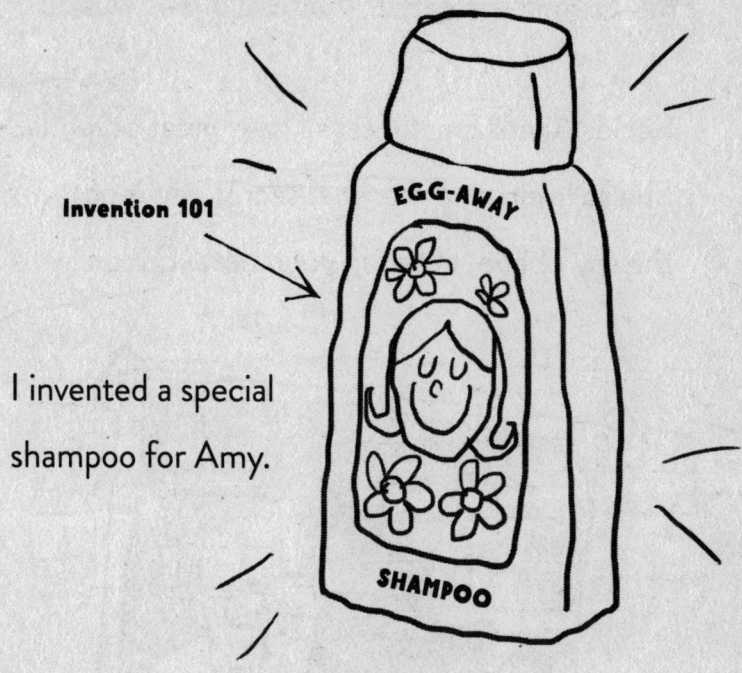

Invention 101

I invented a special shampoo for Amy.

To be honest, I don't think she ever really smelled that badly of eggs, but as long as she's happy, I'm happy.

Now for brilliant thing number 5:

## I'VE BEEN PROMOTED!

Senior Agent Electra says I have great potential.
She still won't tell me what secret info is on
the spy ribbon, but all in good time, Edison.

**Best family** EVER!

Amy's just woken up, and we're going to invent something amazing for breakfast.

**Invention 102 . . . maybe?**

Egg
Mushrooms
Bacon
Sausages
Beans

See you soon, Edison!

Yours inventively

(FOREVER!),

Eliza Boom

Best friend

Dog-Lover

Assistant Inventor

AND JUNIOR SPY

P.S. I almost forgot!

Brilliant thing number 6:

Zoe Wakefield's hair after she'd used my Diva-Pro Ultra-Heated Hair Rollers . . .

# . . . BOOM!

**You can read all about Eliza Boom's next big adventure in . . .**

# Eliza Boom
## #2
## My Super-Spy Diary

Eliza is sure the new neighbor is up to something, but no one will believe her! So it's up to Eliza to invent the one perfect gadget that will help her discover the truth.